D1299582

D.W.'s
Perfect Present

by Marc Brown

LITTLE, BROWN AND COMPANY
New York ✢ Boston

"It's almost Christmas," said D.W. "I know there are more presents for me around here somewhere. And I'm going to find them!"

D.W. started snooping around the house looking for her gifts.
She found Dad in the kitchen.
"Aha!" D.W. shouted. "Is that for me?"

"No," said Dad. "It's for Grandma Thora. She loves my fruitcake."

D.W. kept on snooping.
She found Mom hard at work in the basement.
"Aha!" D.W. shouted. "Is that for me?"

"No," said Mom. "It's a ladder for Arthur's tree house. But it's a surprise. Promise not to tell him?"

"Promise," said D.W.

D.W. didn't give up. She found Arthur
hiding something in the backyard.
"Aha!" D.W. shouted. "Is that for me?"

"No," said Arthur. "It's a giant bone for Pal. He loves to find them and dig them up."

Wow, thought D.W. *That's really nice. Pal loves bones. Arthur will love his ladder, too. And Grandma Thora will love her fruitcake even if it doesn't have any frosting.*

"Wait a minute," D.W. wondered out loud.
"What will everyone love getting from me?"
She hadn't thought about that before.
"It's not too late," she told herself. "I still have time."

D.W. started snooping again. She found all kinds of good things.

Popsicle sticks,

an old photo,

a rubber ball,

an empty jar,

three nickels,

and a candy cane with
hardly any lint on it.

"Has anyone seen D.W.?" asked Dad.
"She's busy with something," said Mom.
"I wonder what she's up to," said Arthur.

"D.W., are you in there?" Arthur asked.
"Yes," D.W. called out. "But you can't come in."
"Are you still looking for presents?" asked Arthur.
"In a way," D.W. admitted.